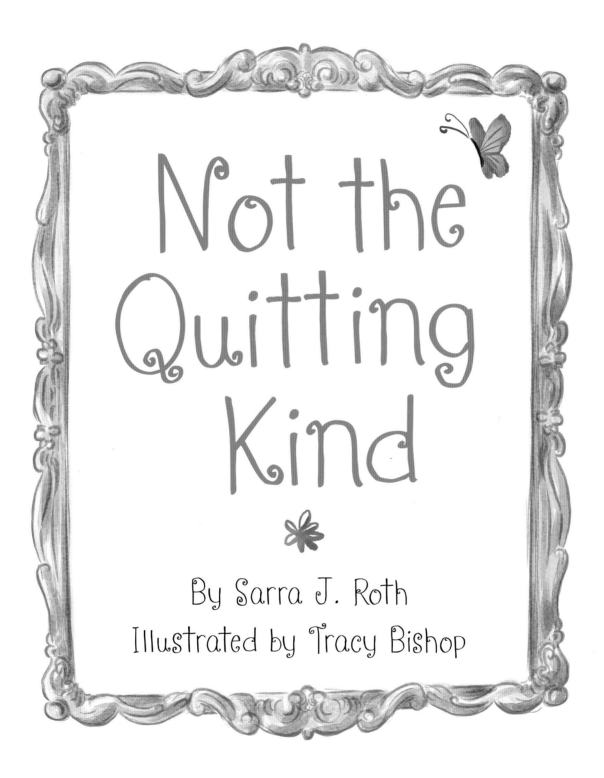

Not the Quitting Kind

By Sarra J. Roth

Illustrated by Tracy Bishop

Peter Pauper Press, Inc.
White Plains, New York

For Andrew, Cooper, and Oliver:
May you never give up
And continue to try.
May you be healthy and strong
And reach for the sky.
– S.J.R.

For John and Andrew
– T.B.

I've been trying out some hobbies,
a few things here and there.
But how come no one warned me
that "first-timers should beware!"?

Like the time I took my bike out,
polished and brand new,

and tried to pop a wheelie
like the other kids can do.

I gave it one strong push,
but my back wheel just deflated.
Now I think that popping wheelies
is COMPLETELY overrated.

I think I'd rather play it safe
to make sure my bike stays shiny,
than risk another wheelie
and end up on my heinie.

So I gave up risky wheelies
for a hobby with more sass,
and walked my new ballet bag
straight to ballet class.

Mrs. Goody Tutu
lined each one of us in rows.
I was the only girl in class
who couldn't balance on her toes.

I was dressed like cotton candy,
and had the clumsiest plié,
so I decided dancing's silly—
especially ballet!

Then I heard at lunchtime,
a friend from down the block
say he had karate
after school at 3 o'clock.

I called my Mom at recess,
and she said I could go too.
But at 3 past 3 I realized . . .

. . . that I really hate kung fu!

My uniform was itchy.
All the shouting made no sense.
I don't see what's so amazing
about learning self-defense.

As soon as I got home,
Mom said, "We have got to talk.
Zipper up your jacket.
We are going for a walk."

She asked about ballet,
about biking and karate.
I told her all those things
can be flushed right down the potty.

"They are boring and they're dumb.
They're not even all that fun.
And while I'm at it, may I mention
that I STINK AT EVERY ONE!!!"

My mom took off her glasses
and looked me in the eye.
"You can't give up so quickly,
after just one teensy try."

"If you walk away too early,
you will fail without a doubt.
In order to get better,
you will have to stick it out."

The next day we had art with our teacher, Mrs. Clay. She said that we'd be making "a glorious bouquet."

I began to paint my flowers,
but they came out way too tall.
I got so angry and just wanted
to crunch my paper in a ball.

But before I got to smashing,
Mom's voice popped in my head,
and told me I should give it
just one more chance instead.

So I picked my favorite color.
"It can't hurt to try once more."
And I made a couple flowers,
each one better than before.

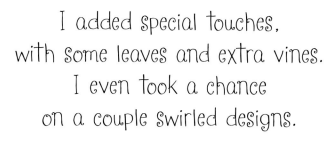

I added special touches,
with some leaves and extra vines.
I even took a chance
on a couple swirled designs.

I finished up my project
just before the end of art.
Did the best that I could do,
and painted from my heart.

I ran my flowers home.
Mommy hung them in a frame.
She even liked the tall ones,
and how no two were the same.

And just as I was leaving
to take my bike out for a ride,
I walked right past my picture,
with new feelings deep inside.

I smiled ear to ear,
and with my newly-opened mind,
decided that I'm never . . .

...going to be the quitting kind.

Published by Peter Pauper Press, Inc.
202 Mamaroneck Avenue
White Plains, New York 10601
U.S.A.

Published in the United Kingdom and Europe by Peter Pauper Press, Inc.
c/o White Pebble International
Unit 2, Plot 11 Terminus Rd.
Chichester, West Sussex P019 8TX, UK

Designed by Heather Zschock

Library of Congress Cataloging-in-Publication Data
Roth, Sarra J., 1978-
  Not the quitting kind / by Sarra J. Roth ; illustrated by Tracy Bishop. -- First edition.
      pages cm
  Summary: "A spunky young girl tries out different endeavors--from ballet to karate--and feels
like she fails at each one. Finally her mother sits her down and gives her the encouragement she
needs to persevere and succeed--and most importantly to not give up"-- Provided by publisher.
  ISBN 978-1-4413-1415-4 (hardcover : alk. paper) [1. Stories in rhyme. 2. Ability--Fiction. 3.
Perseverance (Ethics)--Fiction.] I. Bishop, Tracy, illustrator. II. Title.
  PZ8.3.R7465No 2014
  [E]--dc23

                                      2013031680

                           ISBN 978-1-4413-1415-4
                     Manufactured for Peter Pauper Press, Inc.
                             Printed in Hong Kong

                                 7 6 5 4 3 2 1

                         Visit us at www.peterpauper.com